I0565984

Trapped

Killers Inc. #4

Charity Parkerson

Punk & Sissy Publications

Copyright

—Warning: This book is intended for readers over the age of 18. Some of my books contain allusions to past abuse and trauma.

Editor: BZ Hercules & Consultants

Cover art: Charity Parkerson

Contents

Introduction

RIDGE HAS LOVED HIM since they were kids. Shadow can't stop failing him. There never seems to be a middle ground.

The first time Ridge saw Shadow, he was a goner. They were raised together in a spy program and Ridge had to keep his feelings hidden. Shadow knows, though. He's always known. That's all that matters. At least, that's what Ridge tells himself. Unfortunately, each time he sees Shadow choose a certain someone else, he thinks maybe he hates him a little too. It's getting harder to tell. All he feels lately is trapped.

Shadow doesn't deserve someone amazing like Ridge. He's an assassin. Shadow takes life. That's not the least bit lovable. He should be with someone who keeps him in his place. Ridge needs someone who matches his gentle giant personality. He doesn't understand why Ridge won't give up, but he sees the growing hatred in Ridge's eyes. Sometimes, there are no good choices, especially since he loves Ridge too.

Trapped is the fourth book in Charity Parkerson's Killers Inc. series where hired assassins and their ilk find the love that finally saves them. These are best enjoyed when read in order.

Author Note

THIS SERIES IS ABOUT trained assassins. Assassins aren't born. They're forged. So, this series deals with several elements that shape hired killers. It has darker elements such as abuse, murder, and abduction.

Chapter One

NIGHT AIR BRUSHED PAST him from Ridge's spot on the roof. With his eye to a scope, he watched Shadow move in perfection. Blood flew in a flawlessly planned arch. He heard every sound through his earpiece. Shadow wasn't even breathing hard. His quick movements were from years of practice. Just another job for the entire team. Still, Ridge watched and waited.

All through the mostly silent ride home, Ridge's gaze never budged from Shadow. He knew Shadow was fully aware of Ridge's eyes on him. A few times, they met each other's stare. Shadow always looked away first. He knew why Ridge watched.

They went through the usual decontamination process before heading their separate ways to their bedrooms. Since Ridge's room was just beyond Shadow's, he hung back but never lost sight of him. When Shadow closed himself inside his room, Ridge moved to the door and sat to wait. No doubt, Shadow knew he was there. They always played this game. One day, Ridge would stop. The love in him would die. Not because he couldn't love unrequited any longer, but because Shadow killed it.

These nights were always fifty–fifty. Either Ridge would be the one who comforted Shadow or Zeus would show up, and Ridge would wither a little more inside. When the light went out and the bed creaked with no Zeus in sight, Ridge drew a steadying breath. His place wouldn't be taken tonight.

The moment the first mumbles began, Ridge stood. He slipped into the room and beneath the covers. Shadow muttered angrily in Russian, going over long forgotten orders from their captors. They were children bred for one purpose—to spy for the Russian government. That meant training to fit into any situation and killing anyone they had to kill. Shadow was one of the best, but it came at a high price to his mental health. Except he was the steady one, and so no one noticed that about him. He hid it so fucking well. One of their ground snipers, Field, was the only person on the team Shadow let see him when he was weak. Ridge stole these moments like a thief. His pride had disappeared too long ago to recall. Maybe he had never possessed any to begin with.

When Shadow's words turned angrier and more agitated, Ridge tugged him into his arms.

Shadow reacted the way he always did. He rolled, pinning Ridge to the bed. A knife appeared in his hand and pressed against Ridge's throat. "Who are you? Who sent you?"

"It's Ridge, sweetie. You need to get some rest."

He felt Shadow's muscles relax. A secret wave of disappointment washed over him. In his deepest secrets, he wanted Shadow to slit his throat. End this. As always, that was not what happened.

"Ridge?" The knife disappeared as quickly as it appeared. "I know that name." Every word he spoke was in Russian. He was still trapped in his dreams. "How do you know him?"

"I am him."

Shadow caressed his face. "No. He hates me. He wouldn't come here."

"Where is here?" Ridge whispered the question. He truly wanted to know where Shadow went in these dreams.

"Someplace I would never want him to see." Shadow whispered the answer back, as if afraid he would be overheard.

"Why? He doesn't hate you. He wants to help."

Shadow stroked his face again. "That's a sweet sentiment. You smell like him."

Ridge's chest squeezed. "That's because I'm him." He kept his voice quiet. Ridge couldn't break this spell. This was all he got of the other half of his heart.

"Prove it."

"Just tell me how."

Shadow moved in closer. "Kiss me. He might hate me, but he's the only person who kisses me like he loves me."

"That's because I do."

He heard Shadow swallow. "You have no idea how much I wish that was true. It's okay if you want to pretend."

This was why he stayed trapped in this hell and kept coming back for more. No one knew how he ached for these stolen moments that weren't even real. "I don't want to pretend. I want it to be real."

The air in the room changed.

Ridge knew he wouldn't learn anything else.

"Ridge?" The Russian accent was practically gone.

"Yeah. It's me, sweetie. You were having a nightmare again."

"Oh. Sorry." He obviously still wasn't completely awake. Shadow settled down in his arms, draped over his body like a blanket. He used Ridge's chest as a pillow. "You've always been the most comfortable solid rock."

Ridge shook with silent laughter. He was easily twice the size of Shadow. "My doll. I can carry you around on my hip."

"Sounds nice." Shadow was definitely more asleep than awake. His words were slurred and barely audible.

Ridge kissed the top of his head. "Go to sleep, beautiful. I have you." He always would and it was fucking killing him.

Shadow always pretended to be asleep each time Ridge slipped from the bed. Then he moved into the spot where he had lain and savored the wisps of his scent on the sheets. They were both so fucked up. At least Shadow was self-aware. One of these days, Ridge would find someone worthy of him.

Shadow would continue on in silent agony. It was like they had this pact they didn't speak about.

Shadow checked the clock. It was one a.m. He had plenty of time. After crawling from the bed, he found the clothes he needed and quickly dressed. He sneaked from the room. Since he was a shadow, it was easy. No one ever saw him unless he let them. Once he made it to the garage, he was home free. He jumped into his black MX-5 and was gone. The roads were deader than usual. Most sane people were sleeping. No one had ever accused Shadow of being anything less than unhinged. The tightness in his chest wound tighter as Club Affinity came into view. Really, only the upper foyer was visible. The no-holds-barred sex club was underground. Acts so nasty it would make a heathen clutch their pearls took place right beneath him. Zeus had designed the place to be invisible to any prying eyes. It seemed he had visited a club in Vegas with the same setup and mimicked it. Shadow didn't know why he always came back. That wasn't true. Affinity had one thing he needed: Master Zeus.

Everyone fought to have him. He was a six-foot-six biker Adonis with blond hair and steely gray eyes so light, they penetrated the soul. What no one knew except Shadow was Zeus was also a deprogrammer of former spies. Shadow didn't need to be deprogrammed. He needed everything else Zeus had to offer.

Shadow parked as close as possible to the door. The night air slapped him in the face as he stepped from the car. It never got incredibly cold here, but there was no doubt winter had arrived. Shadow could take it. Russia had been damn cold.

He nodded at the bouncer posted outside. Shadow knew his name, but couldn't recall it. He would make sure he remembered next time. This time around, he was too tired to think clearly. The guy opened the door for Shadow, welcoming him inside. "Have a good time, Mr. Agafonov."

Shadow flashed him a smile and headed in. There were probably people out there who would be ashamed to hear those words. No one inside this club, though. He was only halfway down the stairs before the distinct sounds of sexual pleasure caressed his ears. Shadow had a destination in mind as he reached the long hallway at the bottom. He didn't look right or left as he made his way down the hall. Each room he passed had a different kink on display. Shadow would know. He had been there too. His goal was the doorway at the end of the hall. He pushed, and the sound of loud music poured out. Fog filled the air from fog machines. Different-colored lights bounced in every direction, making everything look slightly psychedelic. Bodies filled the dance floor, grinding against each other. A girl was getting eaten out in the corner while people watched. Typical night at Club Affinity.

Shadow's gaze slid around the room. Zeus was taller than everyone else. Shadow's throat swelled. Where was he? It was very possible Zeus was in one of the many rooms he passed. Shadow couldn't entertain that right now. He had killed too many people tonight. His chest hurt too badly from the invisible weight that never lifted.

Fingers encircled his throat. A hard body pressed against his back. He knew it was Zeus simply by the way he felt hovered over—like a tiny mouse in the clutches of a cat.

"You didn't make an appointment."

Shadow's heartbeat already thumped in his ears. "Do I need one?"

Zeus kissed the shell of his ear. His hot breath had chill bumps dancing on Shadow's skin. "You? Never. But you do have a tendency to assume I'm free."

Irritation stirred inside Shadow. He didn't need this shit. Shadow could go back to his cold bed. He would survive.

Shadow took a step away. The hold on his throat tightened.

"*Nu-uh*. You're in my grasp now."

A soft laugh that sounded evil even to his ears left Shadow's lips. "Don't ever assume you're in control of me."

Firm, warm, and full lips touched his neck. "Stay. Dance with me."

Shadow squeezed his eyes closed. A fresh wave of self-hatred washed over him. There was no reason to go home. He turned, but Shadow didn't meet Zeus' stare. Shadow kept his face turned away as he stepped into Zeus' hold. He didn't want to look into the eyes of someone else he would never have. Sometimes, Shadow wondered if he was the only real thing in a world full of fake people. But when Zeus' warm body engulfed him, Shadow could close his eyes and dream he was... He locked down his mind.

"So, you couldn't sleep again, huh?"

"It's getting worse." Shadow didn't admit weaknesses to many people. Zeus was just one of those people. Shadow didn't have to worry about Zeus's feelings. The guy had none. He was the type of sexy that made the entire world his playground. Shadow didn't matter to him. He could say anything. Likely, Zeus wasn't even listening.

"Come on." Zeus swept Shadow from his feet and headed for the back door. Envious eyes followed every step. The back door led into another hallway. The office was the door on the right. Zeus' apartment was on the left. He turned left.

Zeus barely had to shift Shadow to use his fingerprint to get inside. The lights were out. Zeus didn't bother turning them on as he strode through the living room. Shadow had been there enough times to know exactly how the place looked. Not a single item was out of place anywhere except in the bedroom.

Zeus set him on the edge of his bed. The entire place smelled like his cologne. Shadow wanted to be a bitch and demand Zeus change the sheets, except he knew Zeus. Zeus didn't bring people here. The last thing he wanted was anyone knowing where he lived. He was too in demand. People might do anything to get his attention. Shadow only had it because Zeus knew Shadow didn't really want him. That novelty kept Zeus' attention.""

Zeus took off Shadow's shoes. He peeled off his shirt and took off his boots.

Shadow took the hint. He scooted beneath the covers, leaving room for Zeus to join him. Zeus crawled into the spot next to him and hauled Shadow into his arms. This time, when Shadow closed his eyes in the warmth of familiar arms, it took five seconds. He was out.

Chapter Two

THE WEIGHT ON RIDGE'S chest got heavier by the minute. Since he had woken to the news of Shadow sneaking away in the middle of the night, he had paced the floor. Begged Tracker to trace Shadow's location. Paced some more. Still, Shadow didn't come home. Two hours after nightfall, Ridge couldn't take it any longer. He jumped into his SUV and headed out. Club Affinity always looked dead from the outside. Somehow, they were always still packed inside. He had no clue where all the regulars were parked. Ridge parked next to Shadow's car. Ridge stormed the door, ready to break a bouncer's neck if necessary. He didn't have a membership. Ridge only knew the club's location and schematics because he stalked the fuck out of Shadow. Plus, he wanted no stone unturned when it came to Zeus. No one came near his family without him knowing everything about them, down to their shoe size.

Ridge didn't know what the guy saw in Ridge's face, but he opened the door for him. He gave the guy a sharp nod as he passed. Ridge wouldn't forget the kindness. Inside, he jogged down the steps. His gaze skimmed every room he passed, searching for an unmistakable blond who likely stood a head above everyone. While he saw a lot of things that had him ready to bleach his eyes, he didn't see Zeus or Shadow. He ground his back teeth and pushed through the door at the end of the hall with all the rage in his heart. Ridge dove into the crowd. His head never stopped moving as he hunted his prey. If he had a way to get up high, Ridge would find his man immediately. Unfortunately, he couldn't, and Shadow wasn't his, goddamn it. Finally, he spotted a shirtless Zeus surrounded by men on their knees. Ridge's gaze immediately dropped to eye each man. Shadow had better not be on his goddamn knees for this motherfucker. Thankfully, he wasn't. Ridge would hate to kill Zeus... not really. He would kill the bastard in the blink of an eye if he thought it would make a bit of difference.

Ridge was used to hovering over everyone. It pissed him off to be eye to eye with Zeus.

Zeus didn't look surprised to see him. He pulled the sucker from his mouth, somehow making the move look sultry as hell. Zeus smirked. "Look at you. Flashing eyes. Flared nostrils. Are we fighting or fucking?"

Everything about Zeus was too perfect. It was sickening. "What have you done with Shadow?"

"Nothing he didn't beg me to do."

Ridge ran his tongue over his teeth.

Zeus sighed. "Jealousy. Tiresome. You literally just missed him. Honestly, I don't know how you didn't pass him on your way in."

Probably because he had been searching the goddamn dance floor for ten minutes and Shadow was too good at hiding. Ridge pinched the spot between his eyes where a pain bloomed. He was so tired of living like this. Feeling like this. Shadow made him fucking crazy.

A sharp *thwack* hit his thigh. It didn't hurt, but it snapped Ridge back to attention. It took him a moment to realize Zeus hit him with a crop. "Do you want me to cram that thing up your ass?"

Zeus's eyes swam with laughter. "Kinky. Come with me."

Ridge's tone stayed as dry and droll as ever. "That wasn't an actual offer."

Zeus popped his sucker back in his mouth. "If a single one of you gets off your knees, you'll be banned for a week."

"Yes, sir."

The round of agreements had Ridge fighting an eye roll. Zeus was hot, but he wasn't that fucking hot.

Zeus motioned with his crop. "Move your feet." He used the same hard tone with Ridge as he had with the subs. Ridge didn't know why he immediately obeyed, but he did. Zeus led him to an unmarked door at the back of the club. A fingerprint later, they left the sound of sex and music behind. Another fingerprint and they were inside an apartment. He barely spared the place a glance. Ridge had known Zeus lived at the club. He had never considered what the place might look like. Nor did he care. He was too aggravated to give a damn about much.

Zeus led him into the bathroom.

"I'm not really interested in putting anything in your ass."

Zeus shot him a laughing glance. "You should be so lucky, but no. Come here."

He positioned Ridge in front of the mirror. "What do you see?"

Ridge tossed a quick look toward his reflection. "Myself. Why?"

Zeus rolled his eyes and bodily turned Ridge, so he continued looking at himself. "Look at you and then look at me. What do you see?"

Ridge looked between them. "Yeah. I don't know what you want. It's us."

Zeus released a put-upon sigh. He set his crop on the counter and tossed his sucker in the trash. "Let's play a little game." Zeus stood shoulder to shoulder with him. "You're a sniper. You're observant as hell. I know you can think of something to say other than 'it's us.'"

Ridge took a deep breath and really looked. At that moment, Zeus was a master in his field of deprogramming. He wasn't the guy he played in this club. Well, he was probably that too. Zeus was sexual in every way, but he also took everything he did way more seriously than people realized.

Ridge spouted things off, hoping Zeus got to the point. "You have blond hair. Mine is black. We're the same height. The same size. I don't know what you want."

Zeus smiled for real. He was twice as sexy. "You're getting warmer. We are the same height and build. I bet we damn near weigh the same. Our eyes are the same color. Really look at us. Other than our hair color, we could be twins. Hell, for all we know, we might be. None of us know our true origins.

We are nearly carbon copies of each other."

Ridge looked closer at Zeus and then at himself. Damn. The guy was right.

Zeus held his stare in the mirror. "Why do you think he comes to me?"

Ridge couldn't look away. Zeus could be hypnotic. "I don't know. Probably for all the same reasons everyone here does."

"No." Zeus almost looked sad. "He's not here for me at all. No one here is, honestly. They're all seeking something, but it isn't me. That's especially true for Shadow. With me, he can close his eyes and pretend I'm you."

A derisive snort burst from Ridge. "Is this you hoping I don't take you out when you don't see it coming?"

Before Ridge knew what happened, he found his back against the wall and a very pissed off man had him by the jaw. Zeus looked deadly. His usual mask of calm had vanished. "Do you think I don't want him? Do you think I haven't pulled every trick I know to steal him from your blind ass?" Zeus' thumb skimmed Ridge's bottom lip. He leaned in and swept his lips across Ridge's mouth. To his shame, Ridge was hard as stone. It was more than obvious he stared at the dom who loved control. "I could do things for him you could never dream." He spoke each word close enough to Ridge's lips they brushed his skin. This time, when Zeus kissed him, he went all in. The taste of cherry candy filled his mouth. Ridge wanted to shove him away. He also craved knowing what Zeus had that Ridge didn't. Ridge already knew it was almost everything, but he had one thing Zeus didn't: love. He desperately loved Shadow, and he would stay faithful. Zeus could never, so he supposed that was two things. Either way, Ridge was frustrated as hell.

Zeus pulled away. "Go home. Stake your claim. If you don't, one of these days, he'll submit to me."

Zeus grabbed his crop and walked away, leaving Ridge to silently follow in his wake. He didn't look at Ridge again. Ridge headed for the exit. His mind was a mess. He needed to clear his head. Zeus had given him too much to think about.

Shadow stayed in his head all the way home. He was sick of the drama. More than anything, he was tired of being in love and wanting that love in return. The worst part was, he knew he had it. Shadow just didn't deserve it. Sometimes, he wished he would wake up with amnesia and meet Ridge again for the first time. He wondered how far they would go if Shadow was someone different.

Every day, he watched Ridge's love turn a little more toward hatred. While Shadow knew it was for the best, his heart ached. He wanted back all the moments they shared before Ridge had decided Shadow was a monster.

Blood coated Shadow's clothes and skin. It had somehow gotten into his mouth. God, he just wanted to be clean and for Ridge to hold him. He was more than a little disappointed when he didn't find Ridge waiting for him in the community shower. It was possible they made him stay longer at the shooting range. Fuck. Of all the days for Ridge not to be here, this was the worst. Or maybe it was for the best, all things considered.

Shadow's teeth chattered. He locked his back jaw, refusing to think. Shadow knew how quickly and easily he could fall into shock. He couldn't let that happen. Shadow couldn't show a hint of weakness. Nothing would get him killed quicker. Under the streaming hot water, Shadow squeezed his eyes shut and tried like hell to keep his mind blank. He didn't want to see their faces. They had looked at him and saw a child. He saw the fleeting hope in their eyes that maybe Shadow had been there to set them free. He had been. Just not the way they wanted. His throat got tighter by the second. He wasn't supposed to feel. If he hoped to ever get out of this place, he had to be perfect.

With the blood washed away and his insides shaking, Shadow dried off. He grabbed a fresh robe. Shadow kept his chin up and headed for the room he shared with Rain. Even though Rain was his person, Shadow couldn't talk to him about this. He couldn't talk to anyone. If even an overheard whisper of doubts made its way back to the colonel, he was fucked. All he could do was wait to be in Ridge's arms. That was the only place he was free.

He spotted Ridge heading for his bedroom two doors down from Shadow's room. Shadow couldn't yell his name, but he couldn't stop himself from a stage whisper.

"Ridge."

Shadow watched Ridge's body stiffen in a way he had only seen when Ridge dealt with superiors. A pit opened in Shadow's stomach. He had nothing to go by other than his gut. Then Ridge turned and Shadow saw his eyes. They were dead. No warmth or happiness looked back at him. He didn't even greet Shadow.

Shadow rushed ahead. "Hey. Did they keep you later than usual?"

Ridge's jaw ticked. "No."

The yearning chasm inside him widened. "Okay." He shifted from foot to foot. "I guess I'm just used to you waiting—"

"I saw," Ridge said, cutting off Shadow.

Had he watched? Please God. He couldn't know Ridge saw him—what they made him do. "Oh."

Malicious humor flashed in Ridge's eyes. "Yeah. Oh. Did you get your nights mixed up? Maybe you just forgot to tell Commander Kuznetsov you had other plans."

The confusion cleared. Horror set in. He had been grateful as hell for whatever kept Ridge from coming to him last night. Otherwise, they would have been busted for sure. Unfortunately, he couldn't tell Ridge why the commander had been there. Rain had sworn him to secrecy. The commander had threatened him with a death so horrific, even a heartless assassin like him cringed in fear.

He felt sick. "It's not what you—"

"I listened at the door," Ridge snapped, cutting him off. "I heard his moans."

Shadow snapped his teeth together. He loved Ridge, but he also loved Rain. Rain had been degraded and humiliated enough without anyone else knowing. It wasn't as if anyone had any hopes of stopping it.

He swallowed, fighting back the cries of injustice that choked him. Shadow couldn't look directly at Ridge any longer. If he denied it, Ridge might believe him and put two and two togeth-

er. With nothing left for it, he gave Ridge a sharp nod. With his shoulders squared, he stepped inside his bedroom and closed the door. He kept his movements measured. Shadow might have just lost everything, but that didn't mean he had to give anyone the satisfaction of knowing how much they stole from him. It was officially everything.

The driver's side door opened, making Shadow realize he was home. He had no memory of the drive, nor did know how long he had sat there. Clay went down on his haunches. His hazel eyes looked more than a little concerned. "You good? I knocked on the window a few times before trying the door."

Had he? Damn. Maybe Shadow would finally slip into complete madness. "Sorry. I guess not getting enough sleep is finally catching up with me." Even to his ears, Shadow sounded dead.

Clay held out his hand. "Come on. I'll help you up the stairs."

Shadow glanced around. He didn't want to go back to the emptiness of his bedroom.

"Okay. What would you like to do instead?"

Damn. He was so out of it, he hadn't realized he had said that out loud. "Um. Do you like to dance?"

A bright smile lit Clay's face. He was a handsome guy. Clay looked friendly too. "I don't know how to dance, so it's not really a matter of not liking it."

"Get in. Let's go to the dance studio. Today can be your first lesson.

"Um." Clay let out a nervous laugh. "Are you sure you should be driving?"

Shadow felt lighter by the second. "We're not even leaving the property. Don't be a chickenshit."

Clay's smile somehow got even brighter. "Chickenshit in that accent is actually funny as fuck." He straightened. "All right." Clay closed Shadow's door and circled the car. He jumped into the passenger seat. As if extra proving he wasn't scared, he didn't put on his seat–belt.

Shadow didn't force him. They were literally driving a few buildings over. Shadow just didn't feel like walking that far and he sure didn't want to walk back after dancing himself into the ground the way he planned to do.

At the dance studio, Shadow didn't waste time. He got the music fired up and had Clay tripping around the dance floor in no time. They laughed as Clay stepped on Shadow for the hundredth time.

Clay cried mercy. "Okay. I've made a big enough fool of myself. Let's sit for a minute." He held on to Shadow's hand and moved to a nearby table. Clay pulled out a chair for him before sitting.

Shadow felt better. Lighter. He needed to laugh. There wasn't as much laughter in his life since Field married. The gang's big red-haired jokester was busy healing in the arms of his new husband. Field deserved that. Shadow would survive.

"Is it okay if I ask you a personal question?"

Shadow didn't hesitate. "Of course." Clay knew what Shadow did for a living and Clay was no Boy Scout either. He was an open book.

Clay wiped his palms on his thighs. He looked nervous. "Um. That big blond guy who comes around sometimes. Is he your boyfriend? I'm not trying to assume your sexuality or his. I'm just curious how he fits into your group."

Yeah. Clay was definitely gay. Zeus brought everyone to their knees, eventually. "No. Do you want the absolute truth?"

"Yes."

Shadow was actually having the best time. He liked that Clay didn't know everything about him. "He's a master and owner of a sex club I frequent."

A blush exploded across Clay's face. "Oh."

He was an enigma. The guy worked security for a huge weapons dealer, seeing God only knew what, and he blushed.

Shadow couldn't stop. "You should go sometime. One way or another, you'd have a great time."

Clay's face couldn't get any redder. "Oh. Um. Okay. Maybe one day."

Shadow's face hurt from smiling.

The studio's door was thrown open so hard, Shadow was surprised it didn't come off its hinges. Ridge stormed inside. Shadow watched his long stride and enraged face cross the room, making the space between them smaller. Before Shadow could figure out what he had done this time, Ridge snagged his jaw and hauled him forward. His mouth covered Shadow's in one of the hottest kisses of his life. Years fell away. Shadow tried like hell to hang on to his sanity. He wasn't strong enough to do anything but take it. His heart screamed.

Ridge pulled away, but he didn't release Shadow's jaw. He still looked enraged. "If you ever disappear again like that for an entire night, I'll make Zeus's punishments look like child's play. You're not his. You're mine. If you can't fucking remember that, then I suggest you buy some goddamn Geritol. You do not want me to remind you." He stormed away in the same fury as he had arrived.

Shadow blinked. He couldn't think. His gaze slid Clay's way. "What just happened?" He knew Clay didn't know, but his brain wouldn't work.

Clay smirked. "I think he just threw the ball in your court."

Well, goddamn. Shadow hadn't seen that coming. Now what was he supposed to do?

Chapter Three

IT HAD BEEN THREE hours and Ridge's heart still raced. He had no idea what would happen next. When he had stormed that studio, he hadn't had a plan. His feet had simply carried him to Shadow and his temper took over. Shadow hadn't pushed him away. He touched his lips. Shadow had even kissed him back. God help him. It was everything he remembered. His heart might not survive this. He didn't deserve a second chance.

It had been a month since they left that hellhole. Thirty long days and nights since he learned why Edge had been taken and tortured. Since he had learned the truth about the commander's nightly visits. He hadn't stopped feeling sick since. Ridge could barely look at Edge. Edge had known the commander had been forcing Rain to sexually service him. The guy had known and still he had loved Rain. He hadn't blamed Rain. Edge had passed a test Ridge hadn't. He had been tortured in every way for weeks for his love. Edge was so much more of everything than Ridge would ever be.

Then there was Shadow. Fuck. Shadow had known everything. Witnessed everything. He had been forced to watch and stay silent. Shadow had kept Rain's secret even when it cost him their relationship. How was Ridge supposed to apologize for that? He couldn't. Shad-

ow shouldn't forgive him. He hated this. His eyes wouldn't budge from watching Shadow sleep. They barely had money for a single hotel room. They were all stuffed inside, taking turns getting the beds, but they were warm and could sleep. Ridge was way too close to Shadow. He could make out every flawless detail. Damn. He still remembered the first time he saw Shadow. Shadow and Rain had been doing their ballet lessons since that would be their cover career when they were sent into the world. Shadow moved so flawlessly in time with Rain. He was dark to Rain's light. Ridge had never wanted to be touched as badly before that moment. He hadn't stopped aching since.

Shadow mumbled in his sleep. Several bodies stirred.

Ridge quickly scooted closer before Shadow had everyone awake. He gently urged Shadow into his arms. The sigh of contentment that fell from Shadow's full lips had Ridge going hard. He didn't care about that. They had all been taught iron-clad control. His heart was another matter. The shattered pieces of that stupid organ rattled in his chest. Shadow was supposed to be right here—in Ridge's hold. Ridge had never felt so trapped. He couldn't speak or move. All those years imprisoned, and nothing had ever made him feel this helpless.

Shadow's chin turned upward.

Ridge stared at him, aching. He couldn't stop himself. Ridge lightly swept his lips across Shadow's mouth. The pain that exploded inside him made him wonder *if it was the end. Not a single breath would fill his lungs. The first tear fell, followed by another. He hadn't cried since he was a baby. There was no stopping the flow now. He had lost this, and it was completely his fault.*

For not the first time, Ridge wondered if he had served his time. Maybe he had suffered enough to pay for his crime. Only Shadow could decide, and Ridge had left the choice in his hands. Now all he could do was wait. It was hell.

When Ridge still hadn't crossed paths with Shadow again for the night, he gave up and headed for his bedroom. Shadow's bedroom door was closed, but it always was. He thought about sneaking in, but he couldn't do that. Ridge had to let Shadow make the next move. If

Shadow didn't, then maybe Ridge could finally move on.

He flipped on his bedroom light as soon as he walked through the door. Ridge immediately turned it off again. Shadow slept soundly in Ridge's bed. Ridge ran through his nightly routine, even going as far as to brush his teeth with no light but the bathroom nightlight. He had never been more scared Shadow might disappear. Ridge had also never gotten ready for bed faster. He eased into bed next to Shadow, doing his best not to wake him. When Shadow immediately snuggled closer in his sleep, Ridge's throat swelled. He didn't know what this move by Shadow meant, but it felt a hell of a lot like they weren't over. That was more than he had expected. It was everything he hoped.

A warm body stirred beneath him. The familiar sound of Ridge's heartbeat thumped against his ear. His scent surrounded Shadow. Without an ounce of permission from his brain, Shadow's hand slid across Ridge's perfect stomach. He was scared as hell to hope after that kiss. Ridge had said Shadow was his. Did Shadow want that? Truthfully, he had always belonged to Ridge. It was just that he didn't know how to bridge the gap between them. So much anger and hatred on both their parts had kept them apart for a long time. It had taken

Shadow much longer than he expected to forgive Ridge.

"You should've told me."

Shadow's jaw hurt from grinding his teeth. "I promised Rain I wouldn't. Unlike some people, when I give my word, I keep it."

Ridge flinched, and Shadow knew his words had hit their mark. Maybe it wasn't the same. Shadow didn't know. But Ridge had vowed to love him forever and swore they would marry someday, even if they had to do so in secret. Now look at them. Before Rain's secret came out, Ridge hadn't even looked at him since dumping him. Shadow didn't know how to get past that. He was so fucking angry.

"Do you know the worst part?" Shadow didn't wait for an answer. "Either you thought I would willingly touch that twisted old man, or you didn't care if I was willing. I was still dead to you." There was no way Ridge knew how that realization had eaten at him. He already knew he would love Ridge until the day he died. But Shadow didn't like him any longer and there was no going back. Ridge had killed something inside him.

"I'm sorry. There's no excuse. I know that."

Shadow cocked his head to one side and studied Ridge. All he felt was the same helpless fury he had endured since he watched Ridge walk away.

A sad smile tugged at Shadow's lips. "It must be nice to be you. You get to say *you're sorry and it goes away. But I have to live with everything you broke."*

Ridge looked ready to punch him. "Do you really think this isn't killing me? That it hasn't always wrecked me?"

Shadow took a breath. It sounded shaky. He hated that. Shadow wanted to feel nothing, but this was something he felt all the way to his soul—the betrayal.

"I don't want to fight. It's in the past. You've said your apologies. We can get on with our lives." Shadow tried to walk away. He had ballet rehearsals.

Ridge stepped into his path. "This isn't over. We'll never be finished. Tell me you don't love me anymore and I'll walk away, but I know you still love me. Something this big doesn't die."

Shadow held Ridge's stare. The hope and pain in his gorgeous eyes nearly took Shadow to his knees. "Then walk away, because you killed the love in me a long time ago."

It had been a lie. An angry lie. One Shadow hadn't known how to take back. A new bitterness had grown between them. It had been made so much worse by Zeus. Tracker had been looking for more people like them. He had made it his mission to learn the names of all the spies already launched into society. In Zeus' case, Tracker's amazing hacking abilities had met their match. Zeus had turned up at their door, ready to kill whoever had been hunting him to protect his identity. Shadow had taken one look at Zeus and hope had filled his chest for the first time in years. Little had he known caring for Zeus would be every bit as heartbreaking. It seemed anyone with Ridge's face would crush him.

Each time Shadow held Ridge like this, he felt whole. Every time Ridge pretended it didn't happen broke Shadow a little more. He was scared as hell Ridge would sneak away again, even from his own bed.

"Do you remember the first time we met?"

Shadow smiled at the sound of Ridge's groggy voice. "You were at our lunch table. I couldn't look directly at you when walking toward you. It was like staring at the sun. Yet I couldn't stop my eyes from sliding your way. My body kept moving closer. Then you spoke to me, leaving me with no choice but to meet your stare. I don't even know what you said. All I could hear was the sound of my pulse beating in my ears."

Ridge's body shook with laughter. "I accidentally asked you to sit on me instead of with me. You still said yes."

Shadow's face hurt from smiling. "It's no wonder the rumors about our little group spread like wildfire." They had known they were different. Shadow had known his entire life he liked boys. No one else had known but Rain. Yet somehow, they still found each other. One after the other, their group had gotten larger until they drew too much attention to themselves. All of it felt like a lifetime ago.

"As I recall, I did both."

Ridge shook harder with laughter.

Shadow's throat unexpectedly tightened. "You were the only thing keeping
me going in that place. You were the
only person who saw me. Saw how they
were destroying me with each kill. Now
there's nothing left of me. I'm exactly
what they wanted me to be. Without
you, I gave up."

"You didn't give up. If you had, you
wouldn't be here right now. What they
wanted was someone who couldn't and
wouldn't form attachments. You're attached to this family. They didn't want
you to have the capacity to love. You
didn't lose that. You love me."

Despite the seriousness in Ridge's tone,
Shadow laughed. "What I love is how
sure you are of yourself."

"No. It's not confidence. You tell me in
your sleep."

Shadow's laughter slipped away. "I'm not always asleep."

The whispered confession still hung in the air when Shadow's back hit the mattress. Ridge was on him. His tongue filled Shadow's mouth. Ridge's body surrounded him. Heat seared through him. Lust engulfed him while Ridge tore at the small amount of clothes Shadow wore. He felt too much. Shadow was overwhelmed. He hadn't expected Ridge would touch him again. They were supposed to be over. His heart was even more on fire than his body. All the anger in the world hadn't killed the desperation inside Shadow to be with Ridge. He wanted time to freeze and leave them in this moment.

"Please." The whispered plea ripped from Shadow's soul in between kisses. He wouldn't be whole again until he had Ridge inside him, proving this was real. Shadow still expected Ridge to shove him away and remind him why Ridge hated him. Shadow had done nothing but dig his knife deeper into Ridge's heart since Ridge tried apologizing. He hadn't found the line of hurting Ridge enough to make him feel the way Shadow did. Yet Shadow still felt Ridge missing from him every second.

Ridge shifted positions, settling between Shadow's thighs. "I'm sorry, baby. I don't have any lube or anything." He massaged Shadow's cock.

Shadow would take it. He adored the sensation of Ridge's bare skin against his nude body, but still. "Are you serious?" Why wouldn't he have lube? Then again, Ridge had never brought anyone here. It was possible whoever he went to for pleasure kept everything they needed. Hot coals of jealousy burned in his stomach.

"There's no reason." Ridge never stopped stroking him as he made the confession.

"Why?" Shadow couldn't stop pushing. Maybe he searched for a reason to cling to the armor of his anger. The more Ridge touched him, the more Shadow recalled the heartbreak.

Ridge kissed the tip of his nose before moving to his cheek. His lips found their way to Shadow's ear, making goosebumps rise on his skin. "There's only one you."

No, seriously. There was no way.

Ridge didn't stop. "For me, it was never over." He sucked Shadow's neck and pumped Shadow's cock. "I've just been waiting for your forgiveness." He said the words against Shadow's skin. "I couldn't screw up anymore."

Shadow didn't believe. He couldn't. "You're lying."

Ridge stopped, making Shadow wish he had kept his mouth shut. With his weight braced on his palms on both sides of Shadow's head, he pushed away and held Shadow's stare. The light breaking through around the curtains gave Shadow just enough light to see the truth in Ridge's gorgeous light gray eyes. "You know every need was taken from us. Human connection means nothing to me. You've always been the only exception. You've always been the only one who makes me feel and ache. When I look at you or think about you, I'm someone else. You're the only thing I need to survive."

They had been stripped of their emotions, or at least taught how to suppress them and hide them. Emotions and dependence on any desires got people killed. No attachments. No anything. Just service to their country. But Shadow couldn't call Ridge a liar again. He knew Ridge too well, and Shadow felt the same. Ridge was all he saw in his head. He was the only one who made Shadow feel this way. They knew each other.

"I'm sorry." Shadow's apology came out sounding shaky. He felt closer to tears than he liked. "I never meant to steal your life."

"You didn't. I threw it away when I told you we were over. But I want it back, beautiful." He stroked Shadow's erection, which wouldn't go away with Ridge holding him. "I have to know you're mine. Otherwise, there's nothing."

Shadow ran his hands down Ridge's sides before moving to memorize his chest and abs with his fingertips. "I've been yours since you asked me to sit on you. It seems nothing can break that."

Ridge shot forward and covered Shadow's mouth with his. Talking flew out the window. There probably was a lot of shit that needed to be said. It looked like they had more time for that later. Plus, Ridge no longer toyed with him. There was no teasing. Ridge proved he hadn't forgotten a thing about Shadow's body.

Their tongues battled.

Shadow's hips lifted, seeking more. Every second that passed, he lost a little more control. When Ridge finally tugged him into a powerful orgasm, Shadow lost all control. Pride. Everything flew out the window. A cry tore from him that turned into pleading.

"Holy hell. I want you inside me. I don't give a fuck what it takes. Nothing is right without you."

To his shock, Ridge didn't turn him down with the no lube thing again. He swiped his fingers through Shadow's cum and used it to get Shadow wet. It was hardly enough for this, but Shadow genuinely didn't care. This wasn't physical any longer. He needed the connection. Shadow had to know he made Ridge come. Even though Ridge eased his way inside, Shadow still could barely take him. Just when he thought he had made a mistake, Ridge hit at the right angle and Shadow saw stars.

"Oh my God. Like that. Don't stop. I need to watch you come."

Ridge held Shadow's legs, keeping total control as he pumped inside Shadow. He made short thrusts that kept Shadow completely focused on every minute detail. His fingers dug into Ridge's forearms like he tried to keep Ridge from escaping. When he had begged Ridge to fuck him, Shadow hadn't truly thought he would get a second orgasm. Now he was on the precipice and there was no going back. Shadow stopped breathing. Everything focused on what Ridge did with his dick. When the spring winding tighter inside him finally snapped, a cry tore from his throat.

Ridge lost control. He slammed inside Shadow over and over, riding Shadow's orgasm. When Ridge threw his head back, straining toward the edge, Shadow couldn't look away. He knew the moment would sear into his brain. The knowledge doubled when Ridge blew. He didn't make a sound. Ridge dropped his chin and held Shadow's stare with fire burning in his eyes. That was when Shadow knew it was all true. The love. The waiting. All of it. Shadow would be damned if Ridge ever suffered again.

Chapter Four

RIDGE NEVER TIRED OF watching Shadow and Rain work together. They moved so seamlessly. It was impressive as hell, the way Shadow mimicked every move Rain made, moving in reverse. He knew the flexibility came from years of ballet. That career had been meant to be his cover when they were set upon the world. Watching them, it was magic.

"Are you paying attention?"

Ridge didn't bother looking Edge's way. Edge was his heights-sniper partner, and basically the team leader, but Ridge wasn't dumb. "I know my part. I always know my part."

Edge sighed. It was a put-upon sound. "Do you need to know Rain's and Shadow's parts as well?"

Ridge's gaze finally slid Edge's way. His brown eyes flashed with irritation. That didn't make Ridge want to back down. "Yeah, we kind of do. We're only here if something goes wrong with them."

Edge's features softened. He set his hand on Ridge's forearm. "If something goes wrong with them, Shadow needs you to know exactly how to save him."

Goddamn it. Edge saw right through him, and he was right. Ridge couldn't let anything happen to Shadow. He tempered his tone. "Seriously, I wasn't trying to be an ass. I know my part for exactly that reason."

Edge's gaze moved over his face. He leaned back in his chair. "You're back together."

Ridge couldn't help the smile that exploded across his face. "Maybe."

The way Edge smiled gave Ridge hope. He hated the idea of anyone thinking Shadow was dumb to take him back. They all knew what he had done.

"That's good to hear. I know how much you love him." He should. Edge had been his roommate back in those days.

Ridge nodded. "I'm hoping he doesn't realize what he's done and take it back."

"It won't happen." Edge sounded so certain. "There's no way he would choose this after all these years if he didn't want it." Edge's gaze slid past him. "Speaking of which."

Before Ridge had time to decipher his words, Shadow was there. His fingers buried in Ridge's hair before he tugged, urging Ridge's head back. His mouth covered Ridge's. Ridge forgot where they were. He fully enjoyed the experience with no fucks about who watched. In fact, he had never been prouder. Everyone would know Shadow was his, and Shadow was the one ensuring it.

Shadow pulled away, sounding breathless. "Hey."

Ridge felt how big his smile was. "Hey."

"Are you finished for the day?"

Ridge looked Edge's way.

Edge waved them away. "Go."

That was all Ridge needed to hear. He was on his feet.

Shadow took his hand and headed for the door. "Come on. I have to show you something Clay told me about this morning."

Ridge's eyebrows snapped together. "When did you talk to Clay?" He had no idea why he was suddenly so jealous. Well, he was always jealous, but with Clay? Ridge was fairly certain that guy was straight.

Shadow didn't seem to read anything into Ridge's question. "I saw him at breakfast." He tugged Ridge's hand. "Just come on."

Shadow seemed excited, so Ridge let the Clay part go. The dance studio where they practiced for jobs was a new building on Beau Bosi's property, where they now lived. Beau was a huge weapons dealer. He was rich and dangerous. They needed that last one to keep them safe, so they partnered with Beau. Sometimes they did his dirty work. They got his protection from the Russian government. Shadow headed for another of the new buildings Beau had built since they arrived. Ridge had no idea what was going on. Beau had built five new structures: the studio, Tracker's security building, a garage, and two other buildings he hadn't visited. This was one of those two. Shadow pushed open the door and dragged him inside. It was a house. Large living room and kitchen. Huge bedrooms were on the main floor, fully decorated. He assumed the upstairs was the same. The bedrooms were much larger than the main house where they lived. He supposed Beau had a massive bedroom, but these were different. They were like homes inside a home. It was actually pretty cool.

"Pick a room."

Confusion had Ridge looking Shadow's way. "I already have a room." One next door to Shadow. Besides that, he didn't relish moving again.

Shadow rolled his eyes. "Pick one for us to share."

Ridge froze. He couldn't look away from Shadow. "Are you sure? I don't want you to regret me."

Shadow laughed. His eyes danced with good humor. He looked happy. Ridge could barely breathe. He hadn't thought he would ever see Shadow like this again. Shadow's hands rose and fell. "I only chose the main house to be close to Field, in case he needed me. Now he's married and living with Henry. It's time for us to carve our own space."

"You're really serious." Ridge just couldn't believe it.

Shadow rolled his eyes again and closed the gap between them. He wrapped his arms around Ridge. "Are you trying to talk me out of it?"

"Hell no. Let's take that room." He pointed to the left. Ridge didn't even know if there was a room in that direction. All he cared about was accepting this future Shadow offered.

Shadow shook with laughter. "Okay. Maybe let's find one a little more specific." He kissed Ridge's chest before backing away and tugging him toward the direction Ridge had indicated. Shadow peeked inside the first door he came to and then continued moving. At the second door, he stepped inside. "How about this one?"

Ridge didn't even look. His gaze stayed locked on Shadow. "Okay."

Shadow turned his way, wearing a huge grin. "What color is the couch?"

Ridge shrugged. "Whatever color that has you choosing this life with me."

A bark of laughter burst from Shadow. "That's what I thought. You didn't even look." He reached past Ridge and threw the door closed. "There. We can make sure the mattresses are comfortable."

Ridge shook his head as Shadow headed for the bed with him in tow. "You're always choosing places where there's nothing to make things easier."

Shadow didn't respond. He opened the bedside table and pulled out a bottle of lube. Shadow held his stare as he tossed it onto the bed.

It hit Ridge. Shadow had planned this entire thing. He had already chosen a room for them and set it up to seduce him. "I really fucking love you."

Shadow didn't break eye contact. "I really fucking love you too."

That was good to know. Ridge planned to be inside him soon nonetheless, but having Shadow's love mattered too. He would take that any day.

Shadow loved that he had gotten the drop on Ridge. Honestly, this could have gone any sort of way. It was possible Ridge might not have wanted to move in together. Maybe they weren't quite ready for that. Shadow was, though. He had waited a lifetime to feel the way he did—free from the past. Shadow was ready to only look forward.

The way Ridge crowded his space before taking Shadow down set Shadow's body ablaze. No one looked at him with the same intensity. His starved heart need-ed that insanity. The way Ridge crowd-ed his space said that passion was about to be unleashed all over him.

Shadow didn't have a chance to think a single thought beyond that one. Ridge's lips lightly skimmed his before Shadow found himself with his face pressed into the mattress and bent over the bed. Moans rose in his throat as Ridge kissed and bit his way down Shadow's spine. He tore at Shadow's pants. They disappeared with an ease that should have scared him. Instead, Shadow already leaked pre-cum. He heard the lid pop on the lube. His entire body responded.

"I know you deserve foreplay. Right now, I don't have that kind of patience."

"I don't give a shit. Fuck me." Shadow loved quick results. He was a lot more into pain than he wanted to admit. He had ended up at Club Affinity for a reason. One that didn't completely include

Zeus. Maybe some small part of him thought he needed to be punished. No matter the reason, he moaned from his spot in heaven as Ridge shoved his way inside, thrusting so hard, Shadow's feet left the floor. Ridge knew his body. He knew exactly how to make Shadow fly. It didn't take long at all. The thrusting at the perfect angle had him clawing at the covers and humping the mattress like a whore.

"That's it, sexy. Take it. Show me how you can come like a good boy."

Goddamn. Shadow would die soon.

"You'd better come, Shadow. Otherwise, I might be selfish."

He knew Ridge only tormented him. Ridge would never leave him unsatisfied. But the threat played into Shadow's need for discipline. He fought harder to blow. Rhythmic cries burst from him, tearing from his throat without his permission. His body was on autopilot, fighting its way closer to bliss.

"Fuck, Shadow. You feel so good. Too good. It's almost embarrassing how fast you get me off."

The tension inside Shadow reached its peak. The pressure beating against his crown turned to ecstasy. A loud cry fell from his lips. He broke in their new comforter, blowing cum all over it.

A strangled noise sounded behind him. Shadow savored how Ridge cried his name in pleasure. He felt satisfied in a way he couldn't recall experiencing before. It was like they got stronger each time they touched.

"Fuck. I can't wait to marry you and spend the rest of my life just like this."

Damn. Shadow really wanted that too. It sounded a lot like heaven.

Chapter Five

A MONTH OF SLEEPING with Shadow every night in their new bed had Ridge relaxed in a way he hadn't been ever. When they had been together at the training center, they had been forced to hide their relationship. Then they had broken up before their escape. Now everything was exactly how he always wanted them to be. He couldn't wait to go to bed each night. It was like they had their own cocoon they could disappear to. Ridge was in love with life. He couldn't wait for this job to end.

On his stomach on some random people's roof, Ridge stared hard through his scope at the house next door. This job was different from their usual style. With the guys they were hired to kill working inside a private home, Ridge couldn't see inside beyond through the camera of Rain's and Shadow's masks. He didn't like this. Thankfully, Scout stood outside the back door, waiting to be unleashed. Scout wasn't forced to intervene often. In fact, he didn't even wear a mask. His face was painted like a terrifying clown. That was how rare it was for them to need him beyond scouting the area. He would draw too much attention in a mask. Now he stared into the house through the open door where Rain and Shadow had just made entry. Ridge held his breath. He stared so hard at the dual camera screens, he thought might go cross-eyed.

Shouts were silenced almost as quickly as they came. Blood arced through the air, soaking everything. Then unexpected gunfire cut through the air. Ridge's entire body went on alert.

"There are two guards we didn't know about. I'm going in." Scout disappeared inside the house. More gunfire cut through the night.

Ridge held his breath.

"Area clear. Shadow is down."

Ridge had never been off a roof and then full speed running so quickly in his life. He passed his high-power rifle to the first person he saw. Ridge didn't even slow long enough to see which team member took it from him. He slipped as he flew through the door. There was so much blood. It seemed like every surface was coated in the thick red substance. He righted himself before he actually fell. Seeing the aftermath in real life and not just through a camera made his stomach heave. Since he never saw the carnage afterward, beyond video, Ridge hadn't realized how horrid it was.

Shadow was on the floor in a pool of blood. Ridge had no clue if it was his or one of the eight victims scattered around him. Ridge skidded to a stop on his knees next to Shadow. He felt the rapidly chilling blood seep through his pants. Ridge didn't give a damn.

"What happened?" Ridge frantically searched for wounds. He didn't know why. Rain very obviously held pressure on Shadow's neck.

"We didn't expect to get shot."

Ridge didn't know if Rain realized he yelled. He got it, though. Ridge wanted to rage too. They should have known exactly how many men were inside.

Edge appeared over his shoulder. "We have to move. There's no telling how many neighbors heard that gunfire. The police might already be on their way."

"Is it safe to move him?" Ridge couldn't think straight. Shadow stared at him, wearing an expression Ridge had never seen. It was like he tried to say goodbye, and Ridge couldn't take it.

Their newest team member, Briggs, appeared. "Either we move him or he dies here. Let's go." Before Ridge could rub two thoughts together, Briggs had Shadow in his arms. Rain kept pace with him, keeping pressure on the wound. Ridge had no idea how bad he was. He didn't know if a bullet had torn through his neck or if an artery was nicked. In the face of losing Shadow again, he was useless.

They were in the van and on their way in under a minute. It felt like a lifetime. Ridge held Shadow's hand. Rain silently cried. Tracker called Rain's husband as he drove. He was their physician slash live-in surgeon. They needed him to be ready, if Shadow made it that long.

Ridge couldn't help it and didn't care how many witnesses he had. He kissed Shadow and babbled.

"I love you, baby. Please be okay. You can't leave me again. I might not survive it this time. Just please hang in there. Don't go."

He didn't know if Shadow couldn't talk or if he was too scared to. Either way, Shadow never made a sound. The ride home felt like an eternity. When they got there, everything flew, but still felt like it crawled. Austen had a team ready to go and had Shadow on the table in no time. His brothers kept squeezing his shoulder and placating him. All Ridge could do was wait. He honestly wasn't sure he could survive this.

The curves were tight. Zeus had never pushed his car as hard. He didn't even check how fast he drove. All Zeus knew was he had to get to Shadow.

Field's words still rang in his ears. He had known Zeus would want to know. At the end of the day, he cared about Shadow more than anyone understood. There was nothing he could do. Shadow had the best care money could buy. But Zeus had to be there to pace. If he died, Zeus had to be close enough to touch him. Even he didn't know why. Maybe it wouldn't be real unless he was there. Most everyone didn't feel very real to him. That was a byproduct of being brainwashed by the Russian government. He had dragged himself out of that mess and redirected his rage into control. Shadow was one of the very few people to crawl beneath his skin. He had known Shadow came to him because he loved Ridge, and Zeus just happened to look a lot like him. Zeus still wondered if he had given Shadow his all, if Shadow would have chosen him. Zeus had been too scared to do that, so he had kept Shadow just angry enough with him to keep him from getting attached. Yeah, he was an asshole. Everyone knew it. Zeus didn't know any other way to be. His tires squealed as he zipped into the driveway. He barely had his car in park before he was off and running.

A night guard he had met a couple of times stopped him before he made it to the door. "Ridge might come unglued if he sees you here. He's a man on the edge right now."

Fuck. He hadn't really considered that. "I can't leave." Zeus knew this guy didn't understand. He was connected to this family, even if it was from the shadows. He had to be here.

Clay squeezed his shoulder. "I didn't say you had to leave. You can hang out. I'll keep you posted. Ridge just can't see you. He's not holding up so well."

Zeus nodded and paced. What had he thought coming here would accomplish? The back door opened and ruined Zeus' plan to stay out of Ridge's path. Ridge stepped outside. Their gazes met. Ridge looked like shit. He was covered in dried blood. He looked like a man ready to come apart at the seams.

"Tracker told me you're here."

Zeus nodded. His throat swelled. Ridge walked toward him and somehow Zeus knew exactly what to do. He opened his arms. Ridge walked into them. Zeus hugged him as tight as he could without crushing him.

"He'll be okay. Shadow wouldn't leave you."

Ridge nodded. "He almost didn't make it here. I don't know what'll happen."

Zeus' throat swelled. He couldn't imagine a world without Shadow in it. "He fought too hard to get back to you. You won't lose him." Zeus had no idea if he was telling the truth.

Ridge took a step back. His eyes were red rimmed. "Thank you. I should probably get back inside. Are you coming?"

Zeus shook his head. "My nerves are too shot. I think I'll just stay out here and pace. Clay will keep me updated, but you should definitely be in there, waiting for him."

Ridge took a step back, nodding. "Thanks again for coming. If you change your mind, just come inside. I'm sure the rest of the guys would love to see you."

"I will." He wouldn't. The more he thought about it, the more he realized he didn't deserve to be there.

"Are you two twins? I swear I've never noticed before, but this is the first time I've seen you two this close together. Holy hell. You're nearly identical."

Zeus and Ridge shared a smile. Zeus answered on their behalf. "Maybe. There's no way for us to know."

Ridge squeezed his shoulder, bringing Zeus' focus back to him. "See you soon."

Zeus dipped his chin.

Ridge disappeared inside the house.

Zeus went back to pacing.

"He's lucky to have you as a friend... or brother. Whatever you two are."

Zeus snorted before he could stop himself. "No one deserves the plague that is me darkening their door."

Clay's hazel gaze followed him. "That's not how it looked just now with Ridge."

Because he was an absolute bastard who could have anyone he wanted, he snagged Clay's waist and had him up against his car in an instant. His mouth covered Clay's. Just as Zeus predicted, Clay didn't push him away. He kissed him back. The kiss was—unfortunately—way hotter than he expected. Clay had a talented tongue. Still, Zeus was merely making a point.

He pulled away and held Clay's stare so the guy saw the truth in Zeus' eyes.

"That's all I have to offer anyone, and everyone knows it."

Clay looked unmoved—like the kiss had meant less than nothing to him. "Green Jolly Rancher?"

A smile exploded across Zeus' face without warning. "Yeah."

"I haven't had one of those since I was a kid, and I still haven't forgotten how they taste."

"There's a bag of them in the car, if you want one."

It was the strangest conversation and exactly what Zeus needed.

When Shadow's eyes opened, there was no confusion. He remembered everything, especially the way Ridge had fallen apart. Shadow knew the moment he was awake that he needed to get to Ridge. He tried to assess his situation while fighting against the worst weakness and exhaustion he had ever experienced. A bag of blood hung from an IV pole. He didn't suppose he could lose that. It took a second to realize he recognized the ceiling. With a Herculean strength he didn't really possess, Shadow gritted his teeth and rolled onto his side. There was a surprising lack of pain. He guessed that meant the painkillers were good. Either that or he was dead. If he was dead, he was in heaven. Ridge slept at his side. He looked so peaceful. Gorgeous. Breathtaking, really. That was something that had eaten at his gut when Shadow lost him. To Shadow, there was no one sexier. It had been impossible for him to truly move on. Whenever he looked around, Shadow only saw drab people who didn't hold his interest. Ridge had kept his heart when he had walked away. It had nearly killed Shadow.

"Ridge."

Ridge shot up—fully awake—when Shadow said his name. "What do you need? Are you okay? Are you in pain?"

God, Shadow loved him. "I'm surprisingly not in pain. Austen must've given me the good stuff. Is Rain okay?"

Ridge shook his head. "You scared the hell out of me and you're still more worried about Rain than yourself."

It was true he hadn't asked about his injuries, but he was Rain's shadow. "He has a husband. I wouldn't have been able to live with myself if I had to watch Austen lose him while I lost a piece of myself. When I saw that gun, I just moved, ensuring I was the one who took the hit. Rain has to live. He's owed the happy life he has now." Shadow heard how rough he sounded. His throat also kind of hurt the more he talked.

"What about our happy life?"

Ridge didn't sound angry. It was hurt in his voice. "I knew you wouldn't let me die."

Ridge stared at him as if trying to decide if Shadow was only placating him. "You can't do that shit to me. Okay?"

"Yeah." He heard him, but they both knew Shadow wouldn't stop protecting Rain. "I love you."

Ridge leaned in and pressed his lips against Shadow's. "I love you too. Tell me what you need."

Shadow assessed himself. Ridge wouldn't be happy unless he helped Shadow in some way. "My throat kind of hurts. Could I get some water?"

Ridge immediately climbed from the bed. He wore nothing except his underwear. Even half dead, Shadow couldn't stop ogling him. Ridge helped him roll onto his back again. He stuffed a couple of pillows behind Shadow, making sure

Shadow could drink without spilling his water.

"You're so beautiful. I swear my eyes never want to focus on anything else."

Ridge's mouth lifted in one corner at the compliment. "You don't have to flatter me. I've always been yours."

Shadow waited until he had a few sips before responding. "It isn't flattery. It's the truth. You take my breath away."

A chuckle rumbled from Ridge. "Maybe I should put some clothes on, then. You need every breath you take."

Shadow tried to laugh. It threw him into a coughing fit that hurt like hell.

Ridge tried comforting him. "Austen worried about this. Apparently, quite a bit of blood ended up in your lungs."

"Great."

Ridge chuckled at the sarcasm, but worry still swam in his eyes. Shadow felt a little more guilty by the second. He would find a way to make sure this never happened again.

"Would you hold me? I really need to be held."

Ridge didn't hesitate to climb into bed with Shadow and curl himself around him.

A shiver ran through Shadow. His teeth unexpectedly chattered. "Damn. I'm freezing."

"Austen said you would be weak and cold for a while, considering you lost nearly all your blood. He also imagined there would be a bit of shock."

Shadow kissed the arm that held him. He felt the way Ridge trembled. "You don't have to worry, sexy. I would never leave you."

"Damn right. I won't let you."

Despite everything, Shadow smiled. He had lived. Shadow made a silent vow to savor every moment he got. He had never felt more grateful for the existence he had been given. Shadow would treasure it as long as they lived.

Chapter Six

EVERY STEP SHADOW TOOK felt like death. He was so exhausted, but he tried not to show it. If Ridge knew how bad he felt, he would make Shadow stay in bed. He was bored. Shadow couldn't go back to bed. Instead, he cuddled on the couch with Rain.

"I can't believe I almost lost you. That would've killed me."

Shadow kissed his temple. "Never. I'm your shadow. We stick together."

Rain toyed with Shadow's fingers. "I watched the video. You shielded me."

"That's my job. Plus, I love you. It's always been us—like we're one person. I can't let anything happen to you."

Rain didn't meet his eyes. "Well, Austen wants to give you a medal or something. He's been distraught. He keeps talking about how it could've been me, and his heart can't take this."

While Shadow got it, since he would feel the same if someone kept Ridge safe, no one owed him anything. His motives had been selfish. Shadow didn't know if he could live in a world without Rain. Like he had told Rain, it had always been them. It didn't feel like there could be one without the other.

"Austen doesn't owe me anything. He saved my life. I should think that's good enough."

"Ridge would've gone off the deep end if Austen hadn't. He damn sure would never forgive me."

That was likely true. "And Austen would have never forgiven me if I'd let anything happen to you. So everything worked out for the best."

Rain opened his mouth as if to respond. Austen strolled into the room, pulling Rain's attention away.

Austen was all smiles—like he saw the love of his life. Shadow wondered if he looked like that when he saw Ridge. If so, why hadn't anyone said anything before Shadow lost years he could have spent with Ridge? Maybe he had just needed someone to show him what he missed. Maybe he wouldn't have fought.

"How are you feeling, Shadow?"

"Like dog shit," he answered honestly. "I'm weak, tired, cold, and sick to my stomach."

Austen nodded along with every word. "I'm not surprised. After losing that much blood that quickly, you could feel this way for days, weeks, or even months. The faster you lose blood, the harder it is to recover. I'll give you some prescription nausea medicine. Is it okay if I check your wound?"

Shadow nodded and tilted his head to make things easier for Austen. All he could think was *weeks*? He wanted to get better now. Shadow had already lost so much time with Ridge. Ridge had left forty-five minutes earlier with Edge. It seemed Edge needed help to set up a big surprise for his husband, Mickey. He hadn't said how long they would be gone. Shadow assumed, by the way things sounded, they would be gone for a while.

Austen checked beneath Shadow's bandage. "It's healing nicely." He put the bandage back like it had been, gently pressing the tape back into place. "Now. Will you be okay if I steal my husband? Our dinner is waiting."

Shadow immediately leaned away, freeing Rain. He expected everyone to do the same if Shadow wanted to have Ridge alone. "Of course. I've been listening to his stomach growl for half an hour."

Rain laughed and stood. "Text me if you need me. I have no problem with cuddling with you."

Shadow flashed him a grateful smile. "I will. Go enjoy your husband. You both deserve it."

Rain pressed a quick kiss on Shadow's forehead. "I'll check on you later, babe."

"You're fine. I plan to get as much sleep as possible. I'm wiped."

"Okay." Rain looked understanding. "Love you."

His smile was out of Shadow's control. "I love you too."

With a final wave, Rain took Austen's hand. They disappeared down the hall together. It took all of two minutes for Shadow to be bored off his ass again. He almost sighed in relief when Clay came through the door. He looked more put together than usual. Shadow couldn't explain it. It was like he wore his best outfit or something. Almost as if he had tried really hard tonight to look as gorgeous as he was.

"Hey, sweetie. Are you going out?"

Clay smiled. "That depends."

"On what?"

Clay's smile turned brighter. "If you're willing to join me?"

Shadow searched his mind for a way to gently say no. He felt like shit and his brain wouldn't work properly.

Clay didn't wait for him to work out a plan. "Do you remember how you said I should check out Club Affinity sometime? I've worked up the nerve to go. I'll even drive."

Well, fuck. Shadow had to go. "I'll get my coat."

"Coat? It's still eighty–five degrees out there."

Shadow nodded weakly. "I'm still freezing from the blood loss."

A guilty look passed over Clay's features. "Oh. We don't have to go tonight."

Shadow waved away his words. "You're ready and I'm willing. Let's do this thing."

Clay's smile returned. "Okay."

It didn't take Shadow long to get his coat and shoes. The walk to Clay's car felt like an eternity. He wanted to ask why Clay was suddenly ready to visit a hardcore sex club, but he didn't have the energy to care that much. He just hoped like hell he made it through the night.

The moment Ridge tracked Shadow's location, his temper shot through the roof. The first time he left Shadow home alone, he ran straight to his club. What the fuck? When Ridge left, Shadow had looked to be at death's door. Now he had the energy to go partying. Ridge was behind the wheel of his SUV before he knew what he would do. He fumed all the way there. When he screeched into the parking lot, he parked by the door again and jumped out. The same doorman as last time stood guard. Just like last time, he took one look at Ridge's furious expression and opened the door for him.

Ridge nodded.

Surprisingly, the guy spoke up. "I'm glad to see you. He doesn't look good."

Ridge tried not to show his surprise. He paused and squeezed the guy's shoulder. "Don't worry. I'm about to carry him out of here."

"I'll hold the door."

Ridge had to fight a laugh as he jogged down the stairs. Loud moans and the sound of people being whipped floated through the hall. Ridge had one destination. He pushed through the door to the club. His eyes automatically landed on Zeus. They were both taller than almost everyone inside the place. Their eyes met.

Zeus pointed to his left.

Ridge followed the line of his arm and spotted Shadow slumped over a table. He immediately pushed his way through the crowd, rushing to Shadow's side. "Please don't be dead. Don't be dead." The second he reached Shadow, Ridge felt for a pulse. Relief poured through him when he found it—strong and steady. He kneeled and rubbed Shadow's back.

"Hey, baby."

Shadow didn't open his eyes. "Dear God, please let death take me. I've never felt this horrible."

"It's okay, beautiful. I've got you." Ridge easily lifted Shadow into his arms. As he headed for the door, he looked Zeus' way and gave him a nod in thanks.

Zeus returned the gesture.

Ridge didn't try asking anything until they were free of the loud music. "Why did you drag yourself out tonight?"

"Clay wanted to check out the place." The muttered words sounded like they came from far away—like Shadow was half dead. "He drove, so I thought it would be okay." His eyes peeked open. He met Ridge's stare for a moment. "I was wrong." His eyes closed. "So very, very wrong." He sounded like he might cry. "I didn't tell Clay I was leaving."

"Don't worry, Mr. Agafonov. I'll find your guest and let him know."

Shadow's eyes opened again just long enough to focus on the guy who worked the door. "Thanks, Bronx."

"Anytime."

So the guy had a name. Not that it mattered. He hoped to never see him again. Ridge wished Shadow would be done with this place. He didn't need it. Shadow had him. Anything he craved—no matter how depraved—Ridge would make sure he got it. He had no problem getting as dirty as Shadow needed. He loved everything about Shadow. His twisted side was sexy as fuck, but he got the feeling Shadow hid a lot from him.

Ridge got Shadow strapped into the passenger seat. He quickly made his way to the driver's side and jumped behind the wheel. Ridge turned the heat up on Shadow's side of the vehicle. He went as far as to turn on Shadow's heated seat. There was no missing the way Shadow shivered. Ridge drove home, walking a fine line between getting there as fast as possible and not jostling Shadow too much. Shadow was sound asleep by the time they pulled into the garage. He gently lifted Shadow from the vehicle.

Scout appeared from nowhere and closed the SUV's door for him before rushing ahead to open the door heading into the house. "Whoa. He really looks awful. Should I get Austen?" Scout said the words quietly, obviously trying his best not to wake Shadow.

Ridge seriously considered it before tossing the idea away. "Thank you, but no. I've got him."

Scout nodded. "I know. You have no idea how happy everyone is to see you two together again. There's no one more meant to be."

The words moved Ridge more than he could express. "Thank you for that. He's always owned me."

Scout didn't laugh at the claim, but Scout had always been overly quiet and serious. Only when he was drinking did he brighten.

Ridge stood just inside the doorway and eyed Scout for a moment. "Are you okay? Why were you hanging out in the shadows?"

A smile lit Scout's face, making him look even younger. "You know me. I'm my best self in dark corners. Actually, I was waiting for Clay to get home. I remembered I promised to teach him how to shoot the way I do—fast and accurate."

"No one can shoot like you do."

Scout made a dismissive gesture. "Foster can, but everyone has their thing, I suppose. After all, it was definitely beaten into us. I'm curious if I can teach my method without the pain."

"Baby?"

Ridge dropped his gaze to Shadow, eyeing his pale face. There were dark circles under his eyes. "I've got you."

"I'm cold." A shiver ran through Shadow, as if proving his claim true.

Ridge met Scout's stare again. "It was good talking with you. I have to get him under an electric blanket."

Scout nodded. "When he's lucid, let him know I'm thinking about him."

Ridge gave him a sharp nod. "You've got it." With nothing left to say, Ridge hurried to their bedroom. He wanted to hold and kiss his baby. Truthfully, he never wanted to leave their bedroom again. His heart needed the time with its other half. Life had been too damn hard. For both of them.

Chapter Seven

THE MOMENT SHADOW'S EYES opened, he found Ridge staring at him. He was the best sight to wake up to, but he didn't look happy. Dread rose inside Shadow. He was too warm and comfortable to fight. No doubt Ridge was still pissed about Shadow being at Club Affinity. He imagined it looked very much like he had run to Zeus the first free moment he had. Still, no matter how much he hated it, Shadow couldn't dodge the problem.

"How long have you been staring?"

"All night."

Damn, that didn't sound good. "What's wrong?"

"You ran away the moment I left you alone."

Shadow started to argue.

Ridge kept going, cutting him off. "It makes me wonder why you started going to that place to begin with. What do you find there that you don't think you can get from me? I'm obviously failing you in some way that's more important than your health and life."

Every word he said was ridiculous, but Shadow was too tired to argue, so he went with the truth. A sad smile touched his lips. "Last night, it was totally me doing a favor for Clay. I didn't lie about that. There's no way he knew I felt as bad as I do. You know me; everyone else is always first. I can't seem to stop that. But if you need to know why I have a membership to begin with, I got invited by Zeus to take a tour." In his weakened state, everything felt heavier. He swallowed past the lump in his throat. "Then I was there, and no one looked at me like I was either the enemy or pathetic. No one is judging anyone there. They're just being their authentic self. That's what I couldn't find anywhere else. The moment we burst free from that training camp, and everyone learned the truth about everything that went down in the dark, it was over. Everyone looked at me like I was pitiful. I became a victim in their eyes. Rain was the only one who understood. He was the only person who still looked at me the same. We leaned on each other, but still. Sometimes, I've needed something more. It's not something I can make you understand."

"I get it. From the moment I saw Commander Kuznetsov enter your room, I looked at you differently. Maybe you got so used to seeing my hatred, you stopped looking at me. That made it impossible for you to see the love that stared at you every day. I guess I was just worried I'm not fulfilling something for you sexually. When I saw where you were last night, my heart dropped. I wondered why I'm not good enough. Don't worry about it. I just..." He shrugged.

Damn. Ridge could literally be the absolute worst fuck on the planet, and Shadow would still want him more than anyone. "I hate that this thing happened right when we were getting back on course. Now I can't make you see exactly how much you turn me on like nothing could." Even Shadow heard the lust dripping from each word. Even half dead, he wanted Ridge.

Shadow bit his bottom lip. He felt his expression turned sultry. His gaze slid down Ridge's body. It didn't matter he was underneath a pile of blankets. Shadow knew exactly what that body could do for him.

"Damn. You know I can't resist that look."

A wicked smile tugged at Shadow's lips. "You could do all the work."

Ridge's hand snaked its way out from beneath the hundred blankets Shadow needed to stay warm. He held an open ring box. "You could marry me."

Stunned, Shadow stared at the most beautiful engagement ring he'd ever seen.

Ridge turned visibly nervous. "I know we haven't really talked about it, but this is the life I've always wanted with you. In my heart, you've always been my husband."

Shadow dragged his eyes away from the ring. "When did you have time to buy this?"

Ridge smiled. "Edge didn't really want me to help him plan a surprise for Mickey. It was the other way around. I asked him to go with me to find you the perfect ring."

Shadow went back to staring at the ring. He was blown away. Shadow licked his lips. He had dreamed a million times about Ridge asking him this exact question. Every time, he hadn't been down for the count. He could properly jump him. His gaze lifted again. There was so much hope in Ridge's eyes and a little worry as well. Shadow couldn't have that.

"The first time we spoke, I knew you were the piece of me I'd been missing my whole life. There's nothing I want more than to be your husband, so yes. Of course I'll marry you."

A bright smile exploded across Ridge's lips. "Are you serious? You'll really marry me."

Maybe Shadow was still a little out of it. He couldn't understand why Ridge sounded so blown away—like he didn't know they were meant to be. They were written in the stars.

Shadow stuck his left hand out while trying to keep the rest of his arm covered. "You know I'm yours. You'd damn well better know you're mine. Give me that ring."

With a chuckle, Ridge pulled the ring from the box and slipped it onto Shadow's ring finger. They both spent a moment eyeing it. The piece looked amazing on Shadow's hand. They lifted their chins at the same time. Their gazes collided.

Shadow swallowed hard. He couldn't look away from those sexy eyes. "You know, I was being serious earlier. There's no reason you can't do all the work, while I promise I won't tax myself. It might be the most boring fuck you've ever had, but—"

Ridge overcame him, cutting off Shadow with his mouth coming down hard on Shadow's. A moan escaped before Shadow could stop it. There was nothing better than Ridge's mouth on his skin. If there was, Shadow never wanted to find out. His life was perfect with Ridge.

Nothing tasted better than Shadow. He was like an extravagant meal. Ridge couldn't believe Shadow agreed to marry him. He didn't know why. It seemed like the next logical step, but they had never been logical. They always took the hardest path. Now, he felt higher than ever.

Ridge worked to pull Shadow's pajama pants down enough to free his erection. Ridge had stripped nude in the middle of the night when cuddling with Shadow beneath a hundred covers had him frying. He refused to not have Shadow in his arms—no matter how hot he got. Ridge could just stick one foot outside the blankets.

Shadow wasn't up to getting fucked. Ridge was a little surprised he was hard for him. Exhaustion radiated from him. But Shadow had asked more than once for Ridge to make love to him. Ridge would never make him beg.

Ridge's fingers encircled Shadow's cock. An unsteady breath escaped Shadow. Shadow had a way of taking him from nothing to ready to fly in an instant with a single sound. The feeling never got old.

He held Shadow's stare. "I want to watch you come."

Shadow writhed against him at the claim. "Keep touching me like that and you'll see it sooner rather than later."

Air became scarce as Shadow acted as if Ridge had a magic touch. Ridge pumped Shadow's cock. With his weight braced on one hand, Ridge stared down between their bodies and watched the way Shadow's cock disappeared inside his fist over and over again. There was no way he could handle a long engagement. He was already dying to be Shadow's husband. Ridge was also painfully aroused. He wanted to do all the bad things to Shadow. Possessiveness mixed with lust. Ridge tried breathing past the explosive combo. He had to make Shadow fly. Shadow's fingers squeezed Ridge's bare ass, as if trying to take what he wanted.

Ridge knew how to take a hint. He shifted positions so he could grind his erection against Shadow. His breathing turned labored as he enjoyed the sensation of his dick slipping and sliding again Shadow's cock. He kept control while he stroked their cocks together.

Shadow held tightly to his ass and helped control the pace. "I love you."

"I love you too." He couldn't help but return Shadow's breathless words. Ridge tugged at their dicks, causing the perfect friction between them. He threw his head back and sucked air while driving them both crazy. He massaged and humped, fucking Shadow with no penetration.

Shadow stared at him like he was transfixed.

Every ounce of Ridge's focus remained zeroed in on the sensation of their erections moving against each other. He craved more, but then again, he was happy with any amount of Shadow. Even if he never got to touch Shadow again, there was nowhere he would rather be. There was no one like Shadow for him. As much as he craved burying his dick in Shadow's hot ass, he was completely onboard with making love like this.

Ridge rotated his hips. His speed increased. Shadow's low moans got louder as they raced toward the edge. Ridge couldn't look away and miss a second of watching Shadow relish his touch. The spring inside Ridge wound slowly tighter. His hand kept moving. He needed Shadow's orgasm. Ridge knew it would be sexy as fuck. It always was. Shadow's gaze hit his. His cheeks were flushed, making his gorgeous eyes seem even brighter than usual.

Shadow's bottom lip was held between his teeth. Ridge had never seen a sexier sight. Then, a loud gasp escaped Shadow and hot cum coated Ridge's fingers. The sight ripped an orgasm from Ridge with enough force it tore a cry from his throat. He claimed Shadow's mouth. Their tongues battled as their greedy hearts fought to get closer to each other. The magnitude of Shadow agreeing to marry him landed on his shoulders. This man would soon be his husband. Their lives would likely barely change.

They already slept together each night. They already had the same last name. But Ridge planned to make Shadow so goddamn happy that he saw the difference. For the rest of their lives, all Shadow would know was endless smiles and love. So much love.

Chapter Eight

RIDGE SKIPPED A CIRCLE around Shadow. He was more than a little giddy about Shadow finally being well. Their engagement had him over the moon. He felt like a kid again.

"Tell me my surprise."

Shadow laughed. "No."

Ridge refused to stop skipping. "Please?"

"No."

"Pretty please?"

Shadow grabbed his arm, pulling him to a stop before heading for the door.

"Let's go. I can't have you using up all your energy before we even get there."

Ridge smiled so big, his face hurt. He might have been curious, but really. Ridge loved getting Shadow all exasperated before making him happy again. Sometimes he could be a giant child.

The moment they were on the road, with the darkness engulfing them, all Ridge could do was stare. He loved the way Shadow looked when lights from passing cars highlighted his features. Damn. He was perfect. The image he created kept Ridge distracted. That, and the way Shadow kept kissing his hand. Before he knew it, they were parked by Club Affinity's door. He fought a wave of disappointment. While Ridge didn't know what he expected his surprise would be, it sure as hell wasn't this place. Still, he was with Shadow.

Shadow motioned for Ridge to join him. "Come on. I promise you won't be disappointed."

Damn. Obviously, Ridge hadn't done a good job at hiding his reaction. Determined to take whatever with grace, he climbed from the car. Shadow waited for him with his hand extended. Ridge's mood immediately lifted. He was happy to be anywhere with his other half.

Bronx opened the door the moment he spotted them. He smiled like he was honestly happy to see them. "Mr. Agafonov. Mr. Lion."

The greeting gave Ridge pause. Not only was that not his name, but the guy never hesitated to let him inside. He had to know. "Hey, Bronx. Quick question. Why do you always let me in no questions asked? Not that I'm complaining," he rushed to add.

A line appeared between Bronx's eyebrows. He looked confused as hell. "You're Zeus' twin, correct? He'd have my ass if he knew I denied you entry." His expression cleared. "Not that I'd mind him having my ass."

Ridge laughed. "Yeah, I'm his twin. That makes sense."

Bronx nodded. "You two have fun."

He flashed the guard a smile and headed inside.

Shadow held his silence until they were halfway down the stairs. "Since when are you Zeus' twin?"

A loud laugh burst from Ridge. "I didn't want him to refuse me entry if I need to come get you again. Plus, I really hope he's not my twin. I probably should've said something sooner, but right before we got back together, I showed up here looking for you. Zeus kissed me."

A soft chuckle fell from Shadow's sexy lips. "I'm not surprised. Zeus kisses everyone. It's a hallmark of his personality."

Relief washed over him. Ridge had been scared that kiss would eventually get back to Shadow before he worked up the nerve to confess. He hadn't expected that reaction, but he also had a bad feeling Shadow had done more than kiss Zeus. Thankfully, he didn't have too much time to go down that rabbit hole. Shadow led him inside a private room.

There was a small table with packets of lube and condoms, along with baby wipes. In the middle of the room, there was a swing.

Shadow closed them inside. "I booked the room for a few hours."

Ridge stared at the swing in fascination. He wanted to say he wasn't much into things like that, but the way his dick stirred said otherwise. Ridge could already picture Shadow nude and poised perfectly for the taking. Fuck. Maybe he needed to come here more often after all.

Shadow peeled off his shirt. Ridge's gaze followed as Shadow's hand moved to his jeans. He watched as Shadow slowly unzipped his pants, one tooth at a time. Ridge's mouth watered. He loved a good strip show.

Shadow chuckled. "Do you plan to only watch?"

At Shadow's taunt, Ridge scrambled out of his clothes. He couldn't waste time on any shows. Ridge didn't know how to properly strap Shadow into this swing, but he would damn sure figure it out.

Once nude, Shadow being the strong acrobat he was, easily lifted himself into the complicated-looking device. It was an impressive move, but everything about Shadow blew him away. Shadow leaned back and slipped his feet into two hanging loops. He used a bar above him to get into position.

Ridge decided to act like this was like any other time they made love. Even when they fucked dirty, it was love to him. He grabbed a couple of packets of lube. Ridge used one to ready Shadow's hole and the other to coat his dick. Because he couldn't stop himself, Ridge leaned over and licked Shadow's crown, swirling away the pre–cum. His dick twitched. Ridge straightened and led his cock to Shadow's waiting hole. His insecurities got the best of him.

"It seems like you've used this thing a time or two." He wanted to kick himself the moment the words left his lips. Ridge hated himself a little for ruining the moment.

The flush on Shadow's cheeks and the lust that shone in his eyes screamed he hadn't ruined a thing. Shadow licked his lips like desire made his mouth dry. "No. I've seen it used several times." He gestured upward, pointing out a block style remote hanging above them. Shadow panted for a second before continuing. "If you're interested, you can hit that button. It'll raise the automatic shades between the two panes of glass. Everyone dancing in the club will see us."

His immediate reaction was hell no. The higher his lust skyrocketed, the more Ridge considered the idea. He used the momentum of the swing to pound Shadow. Every sound Shadow made said how much he loved it. Ridge didn't let up. He couldn't. Desire had him in a chokehold.

"You're so fucking sexy like this. Ass all out for my pleasure. Damn. We might need one of these for the house."

Rhythmic moans fell from Shadow's lips.

Suddenly, Ridge wanted the whole world to see them like this. Everyone should witness their love. More than anything, he needed everyone to have no doubt this man was his. If he ever stepped a foot in this club without Ridge, he needed every single one of them to know they were dead if they touched Shadow.

Ridge reached up and wrapped his fingers around the remote. He held Shadow's stare. A pant escaped Shadow. Then he gave a sharp nod, agreeing to whatever Ridge chose. Ridge pushed the button. He tried not to look, but curiosity got the best of him. From inside the room, the window only looked like a mirror. He couldn't see the crowd. But Ridge swore he felt the eyes on them, and he reveled in it. Possessiveness and love mixed with pride and arousal to have Ridge putting his whole skill set into fucking Shadow. The noises he made said he was close. Ridge needed to please him. He had to feel Shadow's hot body trying to milk him to completion.

Ridge struggled so hard for air that he couldn't close his mouth. He swore his eyes wanted to roll back in his head. Beneath his hands, Shadow's body tensed. On a loud cry, cum shot through the air in jets. Pride filled Ridge's chest. He had to keep Shadow to himself. They needed to be alone when Ridge pumped him full of cum. He quickly hit the button above them. Ridge swore he heard loud groans of disappointment. Under any other circumstance, he would be horrified. Nothing could penetrate the desire. With Shadow's hot hole massaging him, Ridge gasped for air as he slammed himself repeatedly inside Shadow. His entire body hardened. Ridge held his breath. The orgasm of all orgasms hit. Ridge cried

Shadow's name. Then he pulled Shadow into his arms, letting cum hit the floor as his dick slipped from Shadow's ass. His tongue shoved its way into Shadow's mouth. Ridge knew right then, more than any other moment they had shared, they would have the most spectacular marriage anyone had ever seen. There was nothing they wouldn't do for each other.

Ridge commandeered his keys as they left the club. Shadow was all contented and ready to cuddle. He practically turned into a cat with the way he kept brushing against Ridge and pawing at him.

Tiny smiles kept appearing on Ridge's lips as he drove. Shadow couldn't look away from the sight of that contented smile while Ridge drove. There was no one more sickeningly in love than Shadow. They were flawless together.

Ridge steered into the empty parking lot of a closed coffee shop. He jumped out and jogged to Shadow's side of the car to help him out. "Come on. I want to show you something."

Since he was willing to go anywhere with Ridge, Shadow didn't drag his feet.

Ridge circled the building until they were in a dark alley. He showed his back to Shadow. "Hop on, spider monkey. Hold on tight and don't let go."

Since he was used to being the shadow no matter what it took, he easily scrambled onto Ridge's back and held on. The moment he was settled, Ridge scaled the building without even losing his breath. Goddamn. That shit was hot. The moment they were on the roof, Ridge urged Shadow into his arms. It took nothing for Shadow to swap positions.

Ridge carried him to a lounge chair that seemed out of place, except the view was breathtaking. He sat with Shadow held tightly in his arms.

Shadow settled in to cuddle and stargaze. He was in heaven. "This is beautiful."

Shadow felt Ridge nod against his neck. "I came here for coffee and to scope out a job just to see if I could make the shot from here. I found this little slice of paradise. You have no idea how many times I've pictured holding you just like in this exact spot."

He was such a romantic at heart. Shadow adored that about him. "What else did you picture us doing?"

He heard the smile in Ridge's voice. "A lot of things, but mostly making wishes on the stars."

Shadow was in love with this conversation. "What did you wish for?"

Ridge chuckled. "A lot of things that have already come true, except I haven't married you yet."

"Ah, I see. These are the lucky stars. Well." Shadow turned his chin up toward the sky. His gaze landed on the brightest fireball in the heavens. "Star light. Star bright. First star I see tonight: I wish I may, I wish I might, have my wish granted tonight."

Ridge chuckled. It was a low sound that caused chill bumps to rise on his skin.

Shadow pressed ahead. "I wish we were at a drive-thru chapel right now so we can get married."

For a moment, the air stilled. It was like the entire universe held its breath. Then Ridge stood so fast, Shadow lost his breath. He was over Ridge's shoulder in a flash. "Your wish is my command." He easily descended the building. Ridge had Shadow back in the car in no time. He pointed toward the glove box. "Is our wedding license still in there?"

Thankfully, it was. Shadow pulled it out to show Ridge.

Ridge glanced over and eyed it for a second. He looked dead set. "Good. Let's go."

Shadow couldn't stop smiling. They had gotten their marriage license only two days earlier. Shadow had chosen to leave it in the car where it had the least chance of getting lost. They hadn't fully decided how to handle a wedding. An actual wedding sounded like time and stress. They wanted it to be quick and something just for them. Ever since Ridge popped the question, they had tossed around a thousand ideas. One had not been a drive-thru wedding. Shadow didn't even know why that was the wish he chose. He was just really ready to do this. Shadow wanted to tell everyone he was Ridge's husband.

The bright neon lights of the chapel came into view. He checked out the curbside wedding's sign. Then his gaze met Ridge's. A silent message passed between them. It didn't matter where they did this. They were ready. In their hearts, this would always be the most beautiful wedding in history.

Chapter Nine

CLUB AFFINITY HAD WAY fewer people inside than the last time Clay visited. Zeus had insisted on throwing Ridge and Shadow a party to celebrate their wedding. He had closed the club for the day and only invited close friends and chosen family. It was fucking torture. All he could see was Zeus. Fuck, he was pretty.

Six-six of solid god in leather. He wore black combats boots and only made eye contact with the person he spoke with. Zeus made people feel seen with those piercing, light gray eyes. The guy dripped sex. He was raw everything. That was what made him such a good dom. When the club was open, a dozen people stayed on their knees with their heads bowed, just begging for Zeus to hurt them. Clay got it. Not the hurting part, but he understood wanting any attention at all from Zeus.

Clay had a hard time not touching his lips. He swore he still felt Zeus' kiss, and it had been months. Zeus had a sensual mouth. Everything about him was like a goddamn Adonis. He had probably fucked literally thousands of people, including one of the grooms. Clay should find that disgusting. Zeus was the kind of beautiful that emptied heads. It might matter afterward, but in his presence, there was nothing that would stop people from dropping their pants.

Lost in his longing, Clay drifted closer. He had no idea why or what he would even say. Clay would fucking die if Zeus knew his thoughts. As perfect as Zeus looked on the outside, he knew it, and that Clay couldn't play into. He had too much pride. Still, as Clay was a foot away from the people surrounding Zeus, nervousness set in. That never went well for him.

A guy regaled the group with stories, holding the people captivated. "This one time—"

Clay's addle-brained tongue ran with his anxious mood. "At band camp," Clay finished for him. Every eye turned his way. They looked at him like he was insane. Not a single person smiled. If Zeus did, Clay would never know. He couldn't make himself look at the blond beauty.

Clay chuckled. "I guess you all haven't seen that one." Clay slowly wandered away, as if he had only been passing to begin with. He spotted his best friend, Fabrice, alongside one of the Agafonov brothers, Scout.

As Clay moved their way, Fabrice's light blue eyes shone brightly with humor. His jet-black hair nearly shimmered under the neon lights. He was the only person Clay ever confided in. That meant he was the only one who knew about Zeus' kiss. It was obvious he had seen Clay actually gravitating toward Zeus. Thankfully, he knew Fabrice wouldn't call him out.

Clay pasted on a bright smile and joined Scout and Fabrice. "What are you two up to?"

They both lifted their cups and answered simultaneously. "Drinking."

"Me too. We should drink together."

Loud laughter turned his head. Field tried climbing his husband's shoulders. "Let me ride you, Zaddy!"

An unexpected bark of laughter burst from Clay. Field was huge. If the giant's husband, Henry, wasn't also built like a brick house, he would be permanently disabled by now.

"Fuck, I'm glad to see that smile be real." Scout said exactly what Clay had been thinking.

"For both of them," Fabrice added.

Clay chose to throw his two cents in, even as Zeus had his eyes sliding his way again. "On God, they both deserve it."

Scout shuffled closer. "Don't let yourself look at him like that. Everyone from the program has a specialty. Zeus was trained to be the seducer. They taught him how to always be the most sensual person in every room so he could get any target in bed. He's considered the leading de-programmer of spies, but some things can't be beat out of us—like my shooting skills. Shadow and Rain's ability to kill perfectly and without conscience is another." Clay turned his head and met Scout's stare. He looked deadly serious. "If you feed into it, he will too. He will seduce you and never think of you again. It's all he knows."

All the guys could be intense. Clay had never seen that in Scout before now. Scout worked with him every day to help him shoot the rapid and accurate way he did. He had only ever seen Scout smile. Before now, Clay hadn't truly noticed how beautiful his eyes were... or how much insanity hid behind them.

Scout didn't stop. "In fact." He took a step closer. Clay had no idea why he didn't take a step back. He also couldn't say why it didn't feel wrong or make him jump away when Scout grabbed the back of his neck and gently towed him forward. He could have stopped Scout, but then his lips swiped across Clay's lips. The next thing he knew, he was trapped in an earth-scorching kiss. Scout's tongue played with his. Clay was completely transfixed. Everything and everyone else ceased to exist. They were alone in the world. Clay's head emptied all thoughts except one: this didn't feel wrong.

Ridge's gaze swept the room. He was almost manic with happiness. Field and Henry were acting ridiculous, or Field was, and Henry openly enjoyed the hell out of himself. A quick burst of soft laughter escaped him as the pair snagged Fabrice and danced him across the floor without an ounce of grace. Ridge couldn't stop smiling at Fabrice's peals of laughter. The young chef was way too serious. The moment passed for him and his gaze immediately jumped back to where Fabrice had stood. Scout openly and possessively kissed one of the Bosi guards, Clay. He didn't look like he intended to let Clay get away. It was nice to see another of his brothers happy.

Speaking of brothers, no matter how over the moon he was, something still ate at the back of his mind. He checked on his husband. The moment he turned his head, Rain dragged Shadow onto the dance floor. Nearly all eyes turned their way. The pair had spent more than a decade in professional stage shows, in the top roles of every great ballet production. It was like watching magic unveil when they danced together.

Ridge took his opening and sidled up beside Zeus. Zeus' eyes weren't on the couple dancing. His stare was locked like a laser on the kiss happening across the room. Ridge chalked it up to Zeus likely having some voyeuristic tendencies.

Zeus not looking at him made it easier for Ridge to speak his mind.

"I think we should find out."

Not only did Zeus focus on him at the words, but so too did Tracker.

Ridge didn't let it bother him. He needed this out of his head. "If you're really my twin, I want to know. I'd love the idea of knowing I have that connection in the world."

Zeus grinned, showing his sexy, playful side. "Are you sure about that? I kissed you."

Ridge shrugged. "You kiss everyone. It's a hallmark of your personality. We can chalk it up to not knowing. Plus, I'm married now. All my kisses belong to Shadow."

Zeus' expression turned serious. His gaze moved over Ridge's face. "Is this really what you want?"

Tracker jumped in. "I could do it for you. That way, there's no fear of your DNA ending up on file somewhere."

Zeus looked Tracker's way. "Seriously? You can do that?"

Ridge didn't hesitate to brag about his chosen brother. "Tracker can do anything. If it involves technology in any way, he could probably do it with his eyes closed."

Tracker's eyes and smile spoke volumes about how Ridge's words moved him.

Zeus chuckled. "Please do it with your eyes open. I don't want anyone coming at me with a cotton swab if they can't see what they're doing. This face pays the bills."

Ridge might have laughed if he wasn't so dumbstruck. "Does that mean you'll do it?"

Zeus brightened. His expression turned genuine. "Yeah. If you're really my blood, I want to know that."

They hugged like they already knew what that test would reveal.

Zeus patted his back. "Look alive. Your husband is headed this way."

Ridge released Zeus and turned. A bright smile snapped to his face. Shadow skipped his way. Sometimes, he was very much a pretty, pretty princess. Tonight, he had that glow.

He hopped in place as he reached Ridge's side. "May I please have this dance?"

Ridge couldn't stop smiling. The gesture felt permanent. He held his elbow out to Shadow. "Whatever my flawless husband desires will be his. Let's go, beautiful." Together, they walked to the center of the dance floor as a slow song began. Ridge held Shadow as closely as he could. He stared down into the face of the one and only love Ridge had ever known. Ridge had never needed more. Even when they hadn't been together, Shadow had been the only one for him. If Shadow ever decided to leave him in the dust, Ridge still wouldn't want anyone else. Some people only got one great love. Shadow was his. If he ever left, be it by choice or death, Ridge would hunt him down. One way or another, it was them for eternity.

Keep an eye out for the next Killers Inc., *Scout.*

About the Author

CHARITY PARKERSON IS AN award-winning and multi-published author with several companies. Born with no filter from her brain to her mouth, she decided to take this odd quirk and insert it in her characters. One of her greatest loves is writing morally gray characters. You'll find them scattered throughout her hundreds of titles.

*Nine-time Readers' Favorite Award Winner

*2015 Passionate Plume Award Finalist

*2013 Reviewers' Choice Award Winner

*2012 ARRA Finalist for Favorite Paranormal Romance

*Five-time winner of The Mistress of the Darkpath

Connect with her online:

*Sign up for her newsletter: https://bit.ly/charityparkersonnewsletter

*Join her readers' group on Facebook: http://bit.ly/CharitysTribe

*Website: https://www.charityparkerson.com

*A list of her social media accounts and giveaways all in one place: http://hy.page/charityparkerson

www.ingramcontent.com/pod-product-compliance
Lightning Source LLC
Chambersburg PA
CBHW070934250626
47159CB00009B/3245